Fangs

Written by Jo Windsor

Rigby

Some animals
have fangs.
Fangs are long teeth.

Fangs can help
animals get food.

fang

Some spiders make webs to get food.

Not this spider!
It has fangs.

The fangs help the spider get its food.

fang

Spiders can get
food with their legs.

They bite the food
with their fangs.

Look at the snake.
It has fangs, too.

The snake can get
food with its fangs.

This snake has a frog.

The snake bites the frog with its fangs.

Spiders and snakes
have fangs to help
them get food.

Index

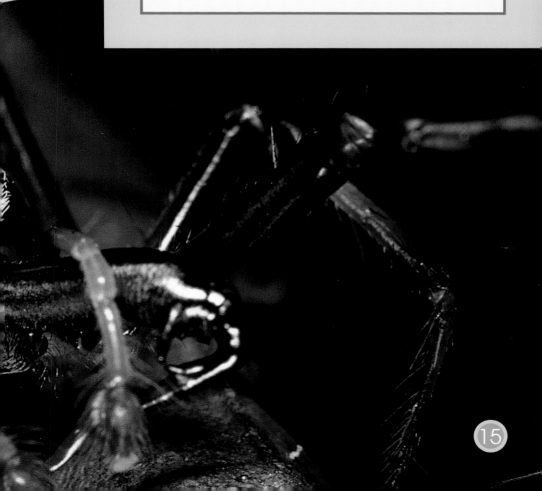

Guide Notes

Title: Fangs
Stage: Early (2) – Yellow

Genre: Nonfiction
Approach: Guided Reading
Processes: Thinking Critically, Exploring Language, Processing Information
Written and Visual Focus: Photographs (static images), Labels, Index
Word Count: 88

THINKING CRITICALLY
(sample questions)
* What do you think this book is going to tell us?
* Look at the title and read it to the children.
* Ask the children what they know about fangs.
* Focus the children's attention on the Index. Ask: "What are you going to find out about in this book?"
* If you want to find out about spider fangs, on which page would you look?
* If you want to find out about snake fangs, on which page would you look?
* How do fangs help these animals?
* How do you think a snake could get food if it did not have fangs?
* What other ways do you think a spider could get food?

EXPLORING LANGUAGE

Terminology
Title, cover, photographs, author, photographers

Vocabulary
Interest words: animals, fangs, teeth, spiders, webs, bite
High-frequency words: some, its, with

Print Conventions
Capital letter for sentence beginnings, periods, comma, exclamation mark